Our Cat Cuddles

Gervase Phinn

illustrated by
Amanda Montgomery-Higham

Published by Child's Play (International) Ltd

Swindon   Auburn ME   Sydney

Text © Gervase Phinn 2002   Illustrations © A. Twinn 2002   All rights reserved

ISBN 0-85953-869-9 (hard cover)   ISBN 0-85953-864-8 (soft cover)   Printed in Croatia

1 3 5 7 9 10 8 6 4 2   www.childs-play.com

Little Lizzie pestered,
She drove her parents mad!
'Oh, could we have a little cat?'
She asked her mum and dad.

'Yes, could we have a kitten, please?'
Her brother Dominic said.
'We really would look after it,
And keep it warm and fed.'

'OK !' said Dad, 'OK !' said Mum. 'We'll get a cat, and so
To the Animal Shelter in the town – that's where we need to go.'

Dominic said :

'I'd like a fat cat, a fierce cat,
A ferocious, catch-a-rat-cat.'

Mum said :

'I'd like a furry cat, a fluffy cat,
A friendly, sit-on-your-lap cat.'

Dad said :

'I'd like a sleek cat, a meek cat,
A lazy, sleep-at-your-feet cat.'

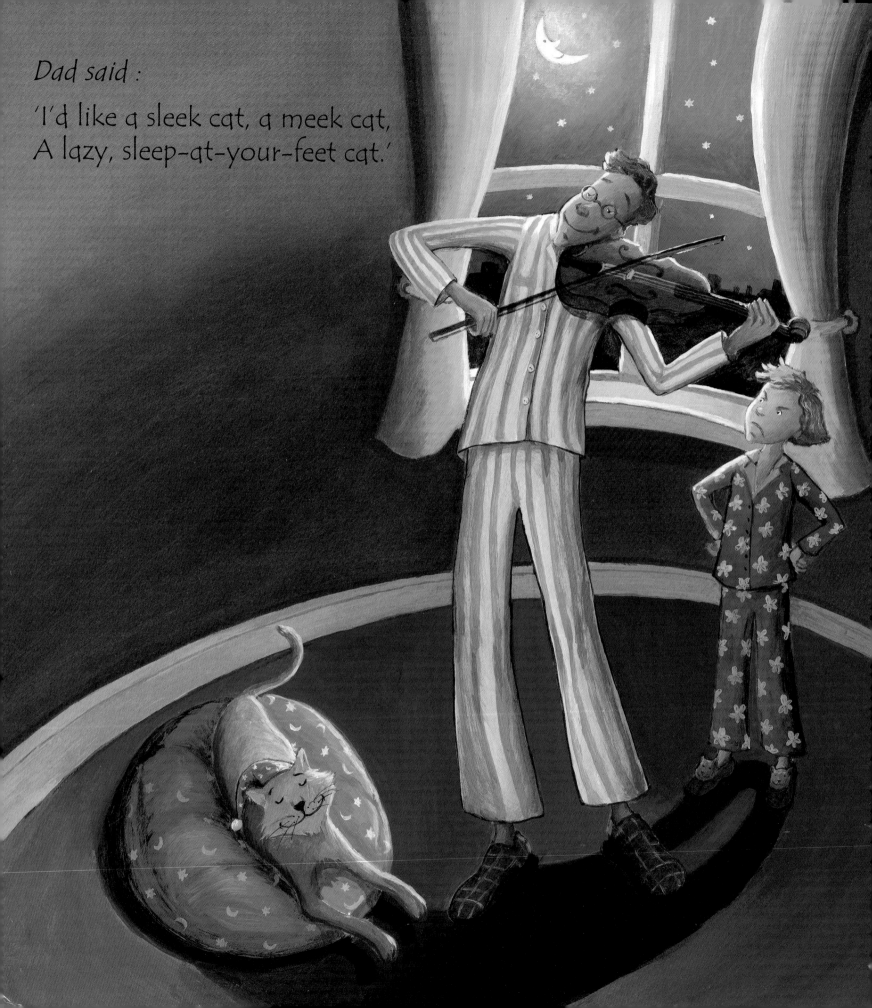

Lizzie said :

'I don't mind, whatever kind,
Will be all right for me.'

At the Animal Shelter they found to their surprise
So many lively creatures of every shape and size:
Foxes, ferrets, pheasants, bats,
Terrapins, turtles, weasels, rats,
Hamsters, hedgehogs, snakes and voles,
Pigeons, parrots, mice and moles,

Horses, donkeys, newts and frogs,
Ducks and drakes and cats and dogs,
Rabbits, lizards, otters, owls,
Gerbils, goldfish, guinea fowls,
Beavers, badgers, squirrels, stoats,
Swans and sheep and billy goats.

Today's Duties

Walk dogs   Flea cats
Find sheep   Wake owl
Mend door   Sweep floor
Parrot talk
Buy phone

'We'd like a kitten, please,' Dad said.
The Keeper smiled and scratched his head.
'What sort of cat have you in mind?
We've every colour, every kind.'

Dominic said :

'I'd like a fierce cat, a fat cat,
A ferocious, catch-a-rat cat.'

The Keeper said :

'We've got tabby cats, shabby cats,
Wild cats, mild cats,
Creeping cats, sleeping cats,
Prowling cats, growling cats,
City cats, witty cats,
Lazy cats, crazy cats,
Shy cats, sly cats,
Spit-you-in-the-eye cats.'

Mum said:

'I'd like a furry cat, a fluffy cat,
A friendly, sit-on-your-lap cat.'

The Keeper said :

'We've got white cats, night cats,
Dancing cats, prancing cats,
Slim cats, trim cats,
Lanky cats, swanky cats,
Frizzy cats, dizzy cats,
Moody cats, broody cats,
Lean cats, mean cats,
Very, very clean cats.'

Dad said :

'I'd like a sleek cat, a meek cat,
A lazy, sleep-at-your-feet cat.'

The Keeper said :

'We've got grey cats, stray cats,
Hissing cats, kissing cats,
Fair cats, rare cats,
Grumpy cats, lumpy cats,
Old cats, bold cats,
Slender cats, tender cats,
Town cats, brown cats,
Jumping up and down cats.'

They looked in every room, and then,
They came upon a wire pen,
And in the corner all alone,
There curled a kitten - skin and bone,
With great sad eyes and matted fur;
They heard its faint pathetic purr.

Lizzie clapped her hands in glee,
'That kitten is the one for me !'

They called him Cuddles, took him home,
And since then he's grown ...and grown ...and grown.

Dominic said :

'It sits in the sun and growls all day,
Then chases all my friends away.'

Mum said :

'It's scratched the curtains into shreds,
It's ripped the sheets on all the beds.'

Dad said :

'It's gnawed the table, chomped the chairs,
It's chewed the carpet on the stairs.'

'Well I don't care,' said Little Liz,
'I like him just the way he is.
He's now got fangs and massive paws,
A shaggy mane and sharp, sharp claws,
Great golden eyes and rumbling growl,
A long brown tail and fearsome howl.

We've had to change his name to Brian.
For 'Cuddles' does not suit a lion!'